FULL MOON
at the
BELL WITCH CAVE

JOY KIEFFER

PAGE PUBLISHING
Conneaut Lake, PA

First originally published by Page Publishing 2023

ISBN 979-8-88960-063-3 (pbk)
ISBN 979-8-88960-073-2 (digital)

Printed in the United States of America

Contents

Chapter 1:   The River 1

Chapter 2:   The Cave 5

Chapter 3:   Time Flies 13

Chapter 4:   Lessons 19

Chapter 5:   Sunday Services 35

Chapter 6:   Dinner on the Ground 39

Chapter 7:   More Ghostly Proof................................47

Chapter 8:   More Lessons...51

Chapter 9:   Steve's Story...61

Chapter 10: Milk Will Never Taste the Same Again 67

Chapter 11: Tinker 73

Chapter 12: Is It Love? 79

Chapter 13: The Witch Hunter 83

Chapter 14: The Outhouse Experience 87

Chapter 15: Andrew Jackson Was Here........................93

Chapter 16: Roots and Dyes 97

Chapter 17: Medicine 105

Chapter 18: The Witch Throws a Party 111

Chapter 19: Time to Go 115

Chapter 20: Home again..119

Introduction

When all your classmates are going to Florida for spring break and you are not, it is hard to be cheerful, but Jimmy gave it the old college try. After his last exam, he walked across the campus to cheer himself up with a pizza from Domino's. As he neared the dorm, Steve Foster caught up with him. He had a pretty lonesome look on his face, so Jimmy invited him to share the pizza. About halfway through the meal, they began to complain about spring break being such a bore when you are broke. Steve scanned the newspaper ads. "I've got it! We will go canoeing down the Red River." Jimmy's first question was, "Where is the Red River?"

Steve picked up the phone and called the Red River Canoe Rental in Robertson County. After a short conversation, he told Jimmy to pack for camping out for a few days.

So that afternoon, they loaded their gear into Jimmy's car and drove north from Nashville. They had everything from bug spray to sleeping bags. Steve was worrying about his grades, especially American history class. He did not see any point in learning how people lived in the old days. As he complained, he scratched and rubbed the wart on his little finger. Jimmy listened and hoped warts were not contagious.

In a little over an hour, they turned off Hwy. 41 onto a gravel road marked by a dilapidated sign, which assured they had found the Red River Canoe Rental. Camping Available. Jimmy just hoped the canoes were in better shape than the sign.

They parked under big trees next to a faded tepee, got out, and stretched as they looked around. There were no Indians in sight. A log building with an inviting front porch had a sign in the corner of the screen door announcing "Office." The man behind the counter was listening to a serious country song, singing along, and beating the counter with pencil drumsticks. He was probably thirty-something and was mighty cheerful for a canoe rental man. When they asked about a canoe rental, he got right down to business, asking their names and addresses and how long they wanted the canoe. He named a price and asked if they would pay cash or by credit card; no checks were accepted. When he was satisfied with the arrangements, he introduced himself: "Mike's the name, boys.

Here's a receipt and a map of the river, and we are ready to load you up." He led them out to an old pickup truck which has several paint colors, none of the original. If you knew what you were looking for, you could read parts of the Red River Canoe Rental sign on the door. They put their gear in the back and climbed in front. Attached to the back bumper was a two-wheeled trailer with canoes stacked on racks on each side.

As they headed south, Mike explained how a country music hopeful turned into a canoe rental man. He must have told the story often because just as it ended, he stopped. Somewhere Mike had turned off Hwy. 41 onto a small paved road, then a gravel road, through a wooden gate, and onto a dirt road. Now they were on the back side of a neglected farm. Jimmy and Steve helped get a canoe off the rack and into the water and loaded their equipment. Mike warned them to stay with the river and not do any exploring on other people's property and promised to meet them as scheduled.

Chapter 1

The River

Jimmy and Steve looked over the river as Mike drove away, canoes clattering. This little river looked about right for two city boys, with no rapids, no whirlpools, and just a lazy stream. They both wore sneakers and cutoff jeans, thinking to get a little sun as they drifted down the river. The next few hours were pure pleasure.

Late in the afternoon, they were getting hungry. When they spotted a waterfall on their left with a gravel bar extending about fifteen feet into the water, they paddled over and beached the canoe. Steve said this was the prettiest place they had seen so far. Jimmy asked if the map showed where they were, but Steve said there was no waterfall on the map. He looked around in the gravel for fossils as Jimmy pulled out the sandwiches, chips, and drinks. You may think that two college students should have known better than to stop here, but neither of them had any idea where they were or what lay ahead.

After making short work of the food, they decided to climb up and see where all that water was coming from. About halfway up the cliff, they found it. The cliff had been rounded out by flowing water, leaving a small hidden spot of land kind of hanging over the river. This was a perfect campsite, so they brought their gear up and set up for the night. As Jimmy followed the water from the top of the waterfall, there was a vine-covered area of a rocky cliff. Jimmy sat down on a boulder and leaned back and farther back until he ended up on his back in wet gravel. The vines closed around him and left him in the dark. Well, not total darkness, but close enough after being in the daylight. Steve came after him and helped him up.

After their eyes adjusted to the dimness, they realized they were at the entrance to a cave; water gurgled through the rocks, and a cool breeze blew over them from deeper into the cave. Jimmy's total spelunking experience was from watching specials on Channel 8. He thought exploring the cave would be fun and told Steve to get the flashlights. Steve was not excited about the idea, but he brought the flashlights and followed Jimmy farther into the cave.

What did you learn in this chapter?

_____

_____

_____

_____

_____

_____

_____

_____

_____

_____

_____

Chapter 2

The Cave

It was late afternoon when they entered the cave. They were about fifteen feet from the entrance when they heard a noise coming from farther back, growing louder and closer. Jimmy felt the hair on the back of his neck standing up and shivers running all over his body. When they saw a huge dark shape coming toward them, Jimmy and Steve fell to the floor as hundreds of bats flew outside to look for their supper. They were lying on gravel, front sides down, in cold water, which is not a comfortable spot to be in. After a couple of minutes, they scrambled to their feet, and Jimmy told Steve that it would be okay now to go through the cave since all the bats were gone. Steve was not so sure, but he stayed with Jimmy.

They walked a few more steps when something icy hit Jimmy on the top of his head, then his forehead; then several drops of water ran down the back of his neck. About then the first cold drop hit Steve's cheek, and he screeched and jumped back. Jimmy shined his flashlight up to the rocky ceiling, and they saw the dripping opening in the roof of the passage, along with a pair of shining red eyes. Jimmy screeched a little himself. It was a big bat, probably the granddaddy of them all, just looking over them as it hung upside down. "Probably taking a shower before dinner," Jimmy said. Steve did not find that amusing.

With thumping hearts, they debated the wisdom of going farther into the cave. But in the back of Jimmy's mind, the word *chicken* kept repeating itself. Out of the corner of his eyes, he saw something move in the shadows ahead of them—not just imagination. Thoughts of bears and wildcats kept jumping around in his brain. For some brave but stupid reason, they walked a little farther into the darkness.

Jimmy's flashlight was skittering around, trying to show them every direction at once as they entered a large room. Steve's flashlight was blinking on and off. Since he had new batteries and bulb, this made him mad, and he muttered something about taking the whole thing back to Walmart if they lived through this stupid trip.

Jimmy was in the lead. As he looked toward another passageway leading from the far side of the room, he saw someone disappearing into the darkness. His fingers fumbled, and the flashlight fell to the ground. Of course, it went out. He yelled, "Hey, did you see that! Someone went in that passageway. I think it was a girl." Jimmy felt around on the wet rocks trying to find his light.

Steve said, "You must have hit your head on a rock. There are no girls in here." Then he shined his light on the gravel, and Jimmy found his flashlight. When he turned it toward the far passageway, of course, it was empty.

The room they were in was kind of rounded, and the floor was in layers like a split-level room. On the left were the highest floor and lowest ceiling. On the right was a ledge below a large opening in the ceiling. There were holes in the walls scattered around, mostly at a floor level. Some were big enough to crawl into, but they were not tempting to either of the boys. There was a cool breeze passing through the room, but that did not account for the sounds. There was a soft whispery noise that sounded like someone or several someones talking in the distance. It rose and fell in a rhythm. They had just convinced themselves that they were hearing the wind when a loud *BAM, BAM, BAM* came echoing around them. It sounded like someone had a big rock and was beating the walls with it. Their nerves were jumping, and they were too. When the echoes faded, Steve said softly, "Just falling rocks." They both tried to believe it.

They moved across the room and into the second passage. About ten feet in, they stopped. From behind them came the sound of another footstep. Jimmy looked at Steve and held up two fingers, meaning *Let's take two steps*. They did, and it did. They stopped, and it took a third step and stopped. This was more adventure than they had bargained for. Jimmy remembered hearing that adventure may be best experienced from an armchair with a book or TV in front of you. Suddenly he understood that idea. Steve said he felt like someone was watching them. Jimmy told him it was that red-eyed bat. They were shining flashlights in both directions, up and down the passage. The shadows of stalactites and stalagmites seemed to move in jumpy circles. On the back of his shoulder, Jimmy felt a hand. Thinking it was Steve trying to settle him down, Jimmy turned to say something comforting to him—only to see that Steve was four or five feet back and looking along the passageway they had just traveled. The hand was gone, and so was every thought in Jimmy's mind.

Jimmy was ready to call it quits when from the back of the cave came the eerie sound of a woman laughing.

Every hair on their bodies stood at attention. Jimmy tried to speak, but nothing would come out. As they stood, frozen with fright, looking toward the back of the passage, a cloud of glowing mist appeared and moved toward them. They both turned, screamed, and ran for the cave entrance. They made it almost into the round room when the cloud caught up with them, passed them in a flash, and disappeared around a bend.

That did not even slow them down. They ran across the room and down the graveled entrance hall, jumped over the rocks, and pushed aside the vines. Somewhere along the way, they lost the flashlights. To this day, Jimmy does not know if they threw them at something or just did not want anything in their hands that might slow them down.

They tumbled out of the cave and landed in the grass. When they were able to get up, they found that their sleeping bags and all their equipment were gone. They looked at the gravel bar below, and their canoe was nowhere to be seen. They were scared, wet, cold, and disgusted. Who could have found their canoe and camping stuff and taken it? They had seen no one since starting the trip down the Red River. Not to mention, how were they going to get out of there, and how were they going to pay for the canoe that disappeared? Since they had no canoe, Steve suggested that they follow a small path to the top of the cliff, find a telephone, and call Mike to come to pick them up. They had had enough adventure.

What did you learn in this chapter?

Chapter 3

Time Flies

When they reached the top, it was later than they had thought. The full moon was shining on trees, grass, a path, and a wooden fence. They followed the path and soon came to a cabin, a real log cabin with a rock fireplace on one end. There were no lights inside, but Jimmy knocked on the door. They could smell the smoke from the fireplace and hoped to find someone around. Not a sound followed their knock. Not a leaf stirred, not a dog barked, and no one answered the door.

Jimmy looked at Steve and shrugged his shoulders. They needed a telephone and something to eat, and a little rest would not hurt. They were tired—being scared wears a person out real quick. So Steve knocked, waited a minute, and then opened the door. There was a little light from the fireplace, and they could see an oil lamp on the table. Nothing electric was in sight, no telephone, no people, just some rough wooden furniture and a quilt hanging down one side of the room. "Steve, look at this. This place is really old. Now I know why they call such old places 'the sticks.'"

As they stepped back from the door, an old woman came around the corner of the cabin and asked, "Who are you, boys? What do you want? And where's your clothes?"

They jumped, and their mouths flew open as they looked at her in disbelief. Steve found enough of a cracked voice to say, "Hello, ma'am. We are lost and are looking for a telephone to call someone to come get us." She looked them over, up and down, and mumbled something about more trouble. Jimmy was nearly six feet tall with straight blond hair and blue eyes. Steve was the same height with light brown skin, kinky black hair, and brown eyes. There was not a lot of light, but they were looking her over too. She was past middle age and dressed in a long worn gray dress; her dark brown hair was sprinkled with gray and slicked back into a knot at the back of her neck.

Steve said, real polite, "Would you tell us where to find a telephone?" She laughed and said it was a little late for that. They would just have to spend the night, and she would get them sorted out in the morning. Now Jimmy and Steve looked at each other, not liking this idea a bit. But somewhere in his discombobulated brain, Jimmy remembered some old jokes about a farmer's daughters. He thought this woman must be a bubble shy of plumb, as his granddad used to say.

Then she said, "Well, you sure look like you need some help, but I'm afraid you won't find no telephone or anyone who can come get you tonight. You boys wait a minute, and I'll light up the lamp." She went inside, lit the lamp, and told them to come in.

Jimmy tried again, "Ma'am, we were canoeing on the river and left the canoe on the gravel bar while we explored a little in the cave. When we came out, the canoe and all our stuff were gone. We do not mean any harm. We just want to get back home."

She barked at them, "You've been in the cave. What did you see in there?" Steve hesitated and then told her about the glowing misty cloud floating from the back of the cave.

She grinned and said, "But it was faster than you, wasn't it? It passed around you and disappeared, didn't it?" Steve asked how she knew about that. She answered, "How do you think you got here?"

Now this conversation was getting stranger all the time. Jimmy said, "What do you mean *how we got here*? I just told you we were canoeing down the river."

She said they were in for a shock and asked them what this year was. Steve replied, "How dumb do you think we are? This is 2010." They looked at each other and rolled their eyes. Steve scratched his temple in a circular motion, indicating that she must be nuts.

The old woman put an iron pot on a hook over the fire and started stirring whatever was inside it. Thoughts of the witch's brew and bat wings ran circles in Jimmy's head. She grinned over her shoulder at them and said, "You ain't as smart as you think you are, and I'm not as crazy as you think I am. This is 1819, and you (looking right at Steve) are in trouble.

What did you learn in this chapter?

_____

_____

_____

_____

_____

_____

_____

_____

_____

_____

_____

_____

Chapter 4

Lessons

Steve turned to face her, his eyes big as saucers. He asked, "What do you mean *in trouble*? We were just canoeing down the river and lost the canoe. We'll pay for it. And where did you come up with 1819? Do you think the canoe was a time machine?"

This brought a short laugh from her. "There are lots of things in this world you don't know nothing about. You think you are smart 'cause you have a little education and your time has more inventions and such like, but you are here now, and here you'll stay until the next full moon." She sighed like she was exasperated with them and their ignorance. "My name is Kate Batts, and I have lived here fifty years and was born on this farm in 1769."

"This was a joke, right? What's next? Candid Camera?"

But she only stirred something around in the pot and turned to set out four bowls, spoons, and cups on the table.

She told them to sit down, and since they were hungry, they did. From a cupboard, she brought a cloth-covered plate of cold corn bread. Then she wrapped a rag around the handle of the big iron pot and set it on the table. The smell was wonderful. Surely there were no bat wings in there. She put a big slice of corn bread in a bowl, ladled some stew on top of it, poured a cup of warm milk, and took it all out the back door. She returned and said, "Dig in, boys. You'll need it."

Without a glance to see what Jimmy thought about this, Steve grabbed the big spoon and covered his corn bread with the stew. Kate and Jimmy helped themselves to the food. By the time they finished eating, they were less nervous and more curious. Jimmy poured another cup of milk and asked Kate what she was doing living here like this. Her answer was short on information. She said, "I'm here to help the fools who stumble through the cave and land back here in time." Then she got up and gathered up the dishes. She dipped water from a bucket into the iron pot and rinsed it around, then threw it out the back door. She put more water in the iron pot and hung it back over the fire.

Steve said to Jimmy, real quietlike, while she was busy, "She must have escaped from a loony bin and thinks she is a pioneer, living here like this. Let's get out of here. We can follow the river, and sooner or later, we have to come to a town." Now Jimmy did not believe Kate could have heard this, but she turned and looked right at Steve. "You could get to Port Royal, about ten miles up the river, but it won't be what you are looking for. It's 1819 in Port Royal too. Nothing there but a trading post."

Jimmy looked all around. Finally he said to Steve, "Hey, I know what's wrong. Did you see any electrical poles or wires outside? Did you see an airplane in the sky or hear a tractor or car on any noise that would be made by machinery?" Steve shook his head. They were pretty much in a daze. Kate asked if they wanted a drink of water. Steve said he wanted a Coke with lots of ice. Kate just gave him a strange look and went behind the curtain made from a quilt. They heard sounds of her rummaging around. When she came back, she asked where they were from. They told her they were going to college in Nashville. Kate grinned and asked, "Is that all the clothes folks wear in Nashville?"

"Well, we have more clothes than this, of different kinds. Some to wear to class, some to work, and some to canoe down the river like what we have on." Kate got a righteous look on her face and replied, "I certainly hope so. You are not wearing much. Folks around here generally wear twice the clothes just for common decency. I am glad my daughter ain't here to see you half naked."

Steve looked insulted. "Where we live, this is not considered half naked. This is what people wear when they are not at work." He rubbed his little finger again.

"Okay," Kate replied. If you are going to be around this part of the country, you better get decent. I have some things in the back that'll have to do. As she went behind the quilt again, Jimmy saw a large trunk beside a small bed. The trunk had a lock on the front. Kate pulled a key out of her dress pocket and unlocked the trunk. She opened it and rummaged around a bit, then returned with two pairs of overalls and two shirts, well-worn but clean. They put them on over their shorts, and the legs were just long enough to partially cover their black Nikes. She gave each of them a quilt and feather pillow, told them to sleep in the loft of the barn, and pointed out the back door. Without a word, they went out.

Sleeping on hay was not so bad, but it was pretty scratchy. It took a while to get settled into comfortable positions. Then they listened. There were lots of little noises that Steve hoped fervently were not made by mice. About the time he started to drift into sleep, something heavy landed on his belly. Steve jumped up, yelling for help, and nearly fell off the loft. Jimmy jumped up, too, and stepped on something that let out a yowl. A huge cat with gleaming yellow eyes glared back at them. It jumped to a rafter and walked across it to the other side of the barn. By the time they got sleepy again, it was nearly time to get up.

The next morning, they woke to the sounds of roosters crowing and cows mooing. They climbed down the ladder and saw an old black man milking a cow. Since they had never seen this done, they moved in for a closer look.

"Morning, boys. My name is Moses," he said with a smile.

"Good morning, Mr. Moses," they replied.

He chuckled and squirted more milk into the pail. "I heard we had company again. Did you boys enjoy your trip?" He started laughing so hard Steve thought he would fall off the little three-legged stool and land under the cow. The cow looked around at him and shifted her feet.

They did not find this so funny. Steve asked, "How did you know about our trip?"

When he got his laughter under control, Moses said, "I know everything that goes on around Adams." So they were in a place called *Adams*. Way back Jimmy's mind, a little bell rang. Adams, Tennessee. What was familiar about that name?

Moses picked up the bucket of milk and slapped the cow on the butt, which seemed to mean *move over* because the cow did. He put the stool on a shelf, untied the rope from the post, and led her out the back of the barn. He took the rope off her neck and watched her walk into the pasture to join her bovine friends. With a big friendly grin, he said, "Come on, boys. Let's eat. I imagine you are powerful hungry."

They all headed for the cabin. Kate was putting food on the table. Moses took the plate she had ready for him and sat on the back step to eat. She told them to wash up outside before they came to the table. They did as they were told. There was a rickety washstand, a bucket of water, and a bar of some rough soap. An old piece of sack was the towel. Meekly they returned to the table.

After a few bites of eggs and bacon, Jimmy asked, "If this is no joke, how do we get back to our time?" With a serious look on her face, Kate looked them over. "As I said, last night was a full moon, and you came through and landed here. Now you have to wait until the next full moon to go back. You're not the first to come through the cave and wish they had stayed on the river, although not everybody wants to leave after they've been here for a while."

Steve swallowed the last bite of his eggs and asked, "What did you mean *I was in trouble*?"

Kate answered with a sparkle in her eye. This is 1819. All the black folks around here are slaves." Jimmy jumped up, his chair fell over, and he nearly followed it. "Steve is no slave. He is my friend and just as free as I am. This has got to be a nightmare."

"Like I told you, my name is Kate Batts. Have you ever heard of me?" She got up and started clearing the table as they sat there thinking. It was right there in front of them, so to speak. Now they knew why the names *Red River* and *Adams* sounded familiar. In grade school, they had to read a book about the Bell Witch, sometimes called *Kate*. All their friends tried to scare each other with stories about her for the next year or so. You know the type. Go in the bathroom, look in the mirror, say *I hate the Bell Witch*, and turn around three times. When you look back in the mirror, she will be there looking back at you. Apparently this woman thought she was the Bell Witch and was still well-known in their time.

Kate brought them back to the *present* by saying, "Well, there's nowhere for you to go, so you might as well be useful. I need some wood cut for the fire, if you ain't too citified." They probably looked sheepish as they got up.

She pointed out the back door toward the woodpile and axe and warned, "You be careful now. Don't cut your foot off. Many a man who has chopped wood all his life has cut his leg with an axe and died from it." Obediently they headed toward the woodpile.

They stood looking at the axe and the remains of a tree that had been sawed into sections. Propped against one section of the big log was a saw with a handle on each end. It was longer than a grown man's arms. Big limbs, little branches, and sections of tree trunks lay scattered around the corner of the yard. Finally, Steve picked up the axe and told Jimmy he would do the chopping. Jimmy suddenly wished he had picked up the axe first.

Steve was standing next to a large tree stump. The top of the stump was level and had lots of cuts in it, which looked like the sharp side of the axe had chopped into it over and over. So Jimmy lifted a chunk of a big limb and stood it on top of the stump. Steve lifted the axe until it was straight above his head. The piece of limb wobbled in Jimmy's hands as he shut his eyes and prayed. When the limb exploded, he jumped back, and his eyes flew open to see what was left at the ends of his arms. Sure enough, his hands were still there. Then he realized that he was not breathing. Jimmy took a deep breath and smiled at Steve, who was looking really pleased with himself. They looked at the piece of wood. It was neatly split into two pieces, one big one and one small one. Jimmy shuddered as he realized that the axe had been less than an inch from his hands. Surely there was a better way, one much less dangerous to his hands. The axe was buried halfway into the stump. Moses ambled over to them and looked at the situation. He stood the larger piece of wood upright and pulled the axe from its bed in the stump. He motioned them back and, with a loose swing, brought the axe directly into the center of the wood, which split obligingly down the middle. He told Jimmy to stand these pieces up and step back. Moses repeated the motion and told Steve that Jimmy did not have to hold the wood every time. Jimmy took another deeper breath and felt that his hands might survive. Steve and Jimmy took turns chopping and stacking for a while.

Kate came out and told them to bring in some wood for the fire, so they each took an armload inside. She looked at the pieces, tried not to smile, and pointed to a wood box near the fireplace. They dumped the wood as she said, "You boys are gonna have the best chance you'll ever get to learn to do some things like your great grandpappies did. Moses will show you how to hitch up the mule to the plow, and you can take it from there. Just be careful. I do a little doc-toring, but there ain't no real doctor for miles around."

They went back outside and saw Moses headed for the barn. He sang as he walked, and when they caught up with him, he said, "Come on, boys. I'll show you around." They followed him into a stall in the barn. "You, boys, watch close now. This here is a mule. That end (pointing to its rear) can kick you so hard your ancestors will feel it, so watch out." They stepped a respectful distance to the side. "Now this here is the other end. It bites. See those big teeth? Watch out for your fingers 'cause a mule's favorite food is a boy's fingers." They did not know how much of this to believe, so they believed it all.

"Now this here is a harness. It goes on his head like this." Moses continued with the instructions, showing them leather straps going here and there, and led the mule outside to a fenced-in lot. There he hooked the mule to a strange-looking contraption, which he said was a plow.

Steve made the mistake of complaining, "This is sup-posed to be our vacation, not more work." He rubbed the wart on his finger again.

Moses said, "I know what a vacation is, boys, and this ain't it. If you expect to eat, you can expect to work. There ain't restaurants or drive-through fast-food places around here, even if you had something to drive."

After a few minutes of absorbing this comment, Steve said, "*How do you know about restaurants and cars and fast food?*" They were really excited, jumping up and down, shoes landing in who knows what. Moses said, real calmly, "You, boys, are not the only ones to pass through the cave on a full moon night. I've been back and forth lots of times. I know lots of things about your time and some other times too."

This was just too much! Jimmy said, "You are kidding us. This whole thing is somebody's idea of a big joke. There is no such thing as time travel. You and Kate just want some free help on this farm for as long as you can keep us here."

Moses grinned. "Have it your way."

Steve asked him to prove it, "Tell us about some other time, something that we would not know."

Moses winked at him, turned on his heel, and did a fancy step. "Hey, bro. Where's your wheels? I need a ride to see my old lady. She's hot to trot, and I've been gone too long. Let's pick up your gal and go to the movie. *Back to the Future V* is on again. I love that old flick."

Steve and Jimmy had heard about that movie which was coming out next fall. One of their friends, Brandon, read the movie magazines faithfully and had told them a few days ago about this movie. It was just not possible that Moses had heard about a movie that was not even out yet. Besides, most likely, Moses could not read.

They must have looked pretty funny, with a stunned look on their faces and their mouths hanging open, because Moses started laughing so hard he fell over onto a pile of hay. When he recovered, he led them and the mule to a field and showed them how to plow what he called a *furrow*. With a lot of *gees* and *haws* and slaps of the reins, he plowed a straight line across the field, turned around at the edge of the woods, and plowed another furrow straight back to them.

He turned the mule around and handed Jimmy the reins. Jimmy thought that did not look too hard, so he took a firm grip on the leather straps and the handles of the plow. They started off a little faster than he had planned, and he plowed the first few feet with his face. When the mule decided to stop and see what the heck was going on behind him, Jimmy got up. Moses and Steve were rolling around in the grass, laughing so hard it sounded like they were strangling. So Jimmy decided he had entertained them enough.

Steve was next at the plow. As he took the reins and handles, the mule looked back at them and seemed to wink. They started off. At first the furrow was pretty straight. Then the mule seemed to get an idea of his own. No matter how many *gees* and *haws* Steve shouted, that mule went where he wanted, which was into the woods. As Steve ran along behind the plow, he yelled, "Hey, stop you no good hammerheaded…!" But the mule ignored him. Moses was sitting under a tree watching and laughing and holding his sides. Jimmy was doing the same. Their sides were going to be sore for several days.

Finally Moses got control of himself and walked across the field to the woods. When he came out, he was leading the mule, and the mule was leading Steve. Steve was all scratched, and his clothes were dirty. He was not smiling, just mumbling and grumbling about mules.

So Moses gave them lessons, teaching them what was meant by *gee* and *haw* as well as how to hold the reins and the plow handles to keep the mule and the furrows going in a straight line. When they stopped to eat lunch, they were exhausted. But through the long afternoon, they kept at it. Steve and Jimmy were glad there was only one plow so they could take turns. When they stopped for the day, the field was only halfway plowed, but they were proud of their work.

They led the mule back to the barn, where Moses unhooked the plow. He sang as he took the harness and singletree off the mule. The mule looked pretty happy about the whole thing, but Steve and Jimmy were too tired to care.

This is how they learned why people in those days went to bed at dark. They were worn out.

After supper they had tried again to get Kate to tell them how to get back home, but she said they would have to be patient and she would help them go back when the moon was full again. They headed for the barn loft and fell asleep on the hay.

Steve dreamed of home and the girl he wanted to date. She was shy and pretty and very, very smart. Jimmy did not dream at all. He was just too tired.

What did you learn in this chapter?

_____

_____

_____

_____

_____

_____

_____

_____

_____

_____

_____

_____

Chapter 5

Sunday Services

The next morning at breakfast, Kate told them to wash up and put on the clean clothes she had piled on a chair. Apparently it was Sunday, and they were going to church. They picked up the clothes and looked them over. They were just like the work clothes they were wearing except cleaner.

Kate drove her buggy. Jimmy rode beside her, and Moses and Steve rode behind them on horses. Steve had never been on a horse before, but he did not have much trouble. They reached *downtown* Adams and rode up to a small building. The yard was full of buggies, wagons, and horses. Kate spoke to several people standing outside as they passed by. She had warned the boys not to say anything more than a *hello*. When they entered the building, Kate told Steve to sit in the back with the rest of the black folks, and she and Jimmy sat farther toward the front.

There were wooden pews to sit on and a potbellied stove on one side near the rough wooden podium in the center for the preacher to stand behind. There were no baptismal, no stained glass windows, and no sound system. About forty-five people sat scattered throughout the room. A man in a black suit stood to start them off with a prayer. Now he must have been taught to be thorough because he prayed for everything from good crops to forgiveness of all their grievous sins. (This, of course, made Jimmy wonder what kinds of sins were available to these people.) The man finally said a loud *amen* and sat down on the front bench. A second man stood up and lead them in a song. He chose "Amazing Grace," and everyone sang their version of the tune. It was enough to make you wonder about God's hearing.

When the preacher stood up, Jimmy could tell they were in for it. The preacher looked so pruned up that a smile would have killed him. He was the most serious-looking person Jimmy had ever seen. He started off reading from some part of the Bible that Jimmy had never heard and then went on to tell them how they were all bound for hell and damnation if they did not repent. This, of course, took Jimmy back to wondering what these people had to repent from. Then the preacher began to inform them of all their shortcomings. It seemed that frivolous thoughts of any kind, anything that was fun, anything that might lead to immoral actions, and being proud of yourself were all sins. So no fun, no lying or cheating, and absolutely no pride in yourself. It crossed Jimmy's mind that the preacher's yelling and quoting scriptures to damn every possible thing he could imagine were probably the only entertainment available to these people. If that preacher could have seen himself up there, arms waving around, frowning and sweating, and carrying on like a crazy person, he might have had second thoughts about his career.

As they left the church, Jimmy heard several men talking about the strange happenings at John Bell's farm. He asked Kate what they were talking about. She told him he would soon see for himself, "We have a genuine haunt in these parts. The Bells have been having troubles all year with strange noises, covers pulled off the beds, and such like. We are all going over there now and have dinner on the ground. You'll get a chance to find out just one of the many things you don't know all about."

What did you learn in this chapter?

_____

_____

_____

_____

_____

_____

_____

_____

_____

_____

_____

_____

Chapter 6

Dinner on the Ground

The first thing Jimmy did not know about was how you ate *dinner on the ground.* A lot of funny pictures flicked through his head as he tried to match that phrase with possibilities. Kate interrupted his musings by telling him that the Bell family had moved to Robertson County in 1804 and purchased one thousand acres of prime farmland along the Red River. They worked hard and were a welcome addition to the little community.

Kate and Jimmy got into the buggy, Moses and Steve mounted the horses, and they all followed a lane to a big farmhouse. This was the largest building Jimmy had seen in Adams. It was two stories in the front, with a one-story addition on the back to one side. Across the front, there were two doors with a window on each side, and a porch went all the way across. A large chimney rose at each side and another one on the back of the addition, probably the kitchen. Behind the house were scattered buildings, some small like an outhouse, some large, probably barns, and in the distance a group of small cabins.

Many other people from church had come over too. In the front yard, tables were set up, and the women were putting baskets and bowls of food on the tables. As they got out of the buggy, Kate pulled a basket of food from under the seat and carried it to a table. Moses wandered over to the side of the house where a group of slaves was setting up their own food.

Steve and Jimmy were left on their own, so they headed for a shady spot under a cedar tree. They did not notice that no one else had picked that particular type of tree to sit under. That day they learned another one of life's little lessons—that ticks like to live in cedar trees. From the limbs, they will drop on you for a bite of dinner, your blood. When Steve saw one crawling on Jimmy's neck, he stared at it, watching it crawl around. Then Jimmy felt a tickle and brushed it off. It landed on his pant leg, and they both watched it crawl toward his feet. Jimmy jumped up and did a shimmy, kicked, and wiggled. Finally Steve pushed him down in the grass and held his leg still while he picked the tick off.

"What the heck was that?" Jimmy screeched. Steve replied calmly, "It was a tick." So they searched each other and found a whole colony having dinner on them. They picked them off, threw them on the ground, and stomped on them. They did not look around to see who was watching them because they were sure they looked as crazy as that preacher. Then, of course, they felt things crawling all over them the rest of the day.

They decided to pick another shady spot and sat on the other side of the Bell's yard, looking around at the people and listening to them talk. Finally Kate called them over and introduced them as "Jimmy, her third cousin's boy, and Steve, his slave." They met John and Lucy Bell, several of their children, and many of their neighbors. Everyone was soon eating, and they made sure to do their share. Those women could really cook!

In case you did not know, the dinner is not really on the ground. The food was on tables, and they all walked around filling their plates. There being a shortage of chairs, they sat on the ground while they ate.

Steve commented quietly, "If our teachers could hear how these people butcher the English language, they would have a fit." Jimmy was not concerned about their teachers and wondered if they would ever see them again. He told

Steve that if this was a practical joke, it was the best one that had ever been played. Jimmy said he was beginning to believe that the cave was a time machine and they were definitely in trouble. Steve said, "What do you mean by 'we'? I am several shades darker than you, and all the other darkies are eating over by the barn." He again scratched the wart on his finger. It was driving him crazy.

After everyone had eaten, and let me tell you those folks could put away an amazing amount of food, they gathered on and around the porch to sing. The preacher started off with a prayer. Since Jimmy was peeping, he was the only one to see a platter of turkey bones start to quiver on the table. Then it floated through the air and stopped right over the preacher's head. When he finished the "blessing," everyone looked up and gasped. Some of the women screamed, and a man shouted to him to look out. Just as the preacher looked up, the platter turned over. Turkey bones and grease landed on his head and dropped all over his clothes. The sound of a woman's laughter seemed to come from the air around the tables. That eerie laugh was familiar.

Kate walked a few steps over to them and asked, "Well, now, boys, what do you think of that?" Steve just could not believe it. He stuttered, "What happened? Did you see that platter floating over his head and turn over?" Jimmy just shook his head as he looked at the platter which was now behaving like a platter, lying quietly on the ground at the foot of the porch steps.

People in the yard were looking either scared or angry, as their temperaments indicated. Some of the men were talking about ways to get rid of the spirit, but they could not agree on a plan. The preacher wiped his clothes and head fairly free of grease, and now he was angry. He knew this was a direct insult to him, his powers, and his God. He decided it was time to get rid of this spirit, for sure. So he beat a spoon against a pan until they all got quiet. He suggested that God's powers were stronger than any spirit, and if they all sang and prayed together, it would be too much for the evil spirit.

So they sang and sang and prayed and prayed. Some woman's voice was singing the loudest of all. When they realized that the voice was coming from above them, they looked for the singer, but it was useless. It was the spirit, and she was in a good voice that day. When the preacher prayed, hers was the loudest *amen* they heard.

As the afternoon wore on, clouds gathered in the west and headed their way. The wind picked up, and they had to scramble to gather their baskets and other belongings.

As people headed for their wagons and buggies, lightning streaked across the sky. They were too late. Rain fell by the bucketful, so Kate, Steve, and Jimmy joined those headed into the house.

What did you learn in this chapter?

Chapter 7

More Ghostly Proof

They crowded into the parlor and dried off near the fireplace. Lucy Bell served hot peppermint tea and suggested they sing their favorite hymns. One of the ladies played the upright piano as they sang "Rock of Ages." Jimmy had to admit that some had more enthusiasm than singing ability. As they finished, a gust of cold air blew through the room. The doors and windows were closed, but the parlor fire flared up, and sparks flew. The candles fluttered and went out. The lady at the piano jumped up from the bench and ran to her husband. All eyes turned toward the piano as it began to play itself. They could see the keys being pressed, but no one was visible. The same eerie laugh filled the room, and every hair on Jimmy's body stood at attention—again. Several of the ladies fell into the arms of the nearest male, needing their strong arms to keep them from falling onto the floor in a heap. Some of the men did not look so steady either. Confusion and fright took over the small group. Mr. Bell tiredly suggested that they end the evening because it was getting late.

Earlier in the afternoon as they ate in the Bell's yard, Steve and Jimmy had talked in whispers about getting out of this crazy place later that very night. They knew that Kate was too far away to have overheard them, but she seemed to know what they were planning. Kate walked over to Mr. Bell, and they talked softly while glancing at the boys several times.

When Jimmy followed Kate from the parlor, Mr. Bell told Steve to come with him out the back of the house. Kate and Jimmy climbed into the buggy. She told him that Steve would not be coming with them. She had loaned him to John Bell to help with the planting. Jimmy was furious and refused to talk to her. She explained that she knew about their plan and that they could not be allowed to leave until the next full moon if they really wanted to go back to their homes. Jimmy ranted and raved a bit, but she said this was the only way she could think of to keep them here.

The ride back to Kate's cabin was the longest ride Jimmy had ever taken, sitting in that buggy in the dark, in the drizzling rain, without his only friend. He knew Steve was mad and lonely, too.

When he lay down in the hayloft, Jimmy thought about the stories of the Bell Witch, the floating platter dumping greasy turkey bones on the preacher, and the piano that played itself. Then there was that voice and the strange laughter. Maybe Kate was right—there were lots of things he did not know about.

What did you learn in this chapter?

_____

_____

_____

_____

_____

_____

_____

_____

_____

_____

_____

_____

Chapter 8

More Lessons

On Monday morning, Jimmy got his next lesson when Kate told him to take a basket and gather the eggs. He approached the chicken house slowly, thankful that the chickens and rooster were already scattered around the yard and woods. When he pulled the door open, the odor hit him like a fist. He turned his head away and took a deep breath. His first steps were hesitant because he knew what he was walking on. He reached out slowly and grabbed an egg from the nest. As he continued down the row, carefully putting the eggs in the basket, he realized that the eggs had something sticky and green on them here and there. This almost made him drop the basket. Still trying not to breathe, he grabbed the last egg and turned for the door. His foot slipped in the slimy mess on the dirt floor, and he fell onto his butt, somehow holding the basket of eggs up so they were not broken. He grabbed the edge of the rough shelf that held the nests and got up slowly. Nearly in tears, either from the smell or from embarrassment, he carefully scooted across the little room and shut the door behind him. Phew! He smelled so bad. The seat of his overalls was covered in chicken poop, which he discovered when he swiped his hand across his butt. His shoes had a layer too. The only thing he could do was get out of his shoes and overalls.

When he walked into the cabin and handed the basket to Kate, she was stymied. "Where's your britches and shoes?"

Jimmy had no choice but to tell her what happened. She laughed and laughed. Poor Jimmy just stood there until she got a grip on herself. She went behind the quilt curtain and brought him another old slightly ragged pair of overalls, which he put on over his shorts and shirt. Kate said she would clean off the eggs and sent Jimmy to the barn.

Moses took Jimmy and the mule back to the field they had started plowing on Saturday. They finished by noon and came to the cabin to eat lunch. Jimmy was hoping they could go fishing, but Moses just led him to the south side of the barn, where some strange boxy shapes were lined up in rows on the ground. He told Jimmy these were called cold frames and showed him the small plants inside them.

Kate joined them, and they carefully dug up the plants, laying them in big flat baskets. Jimmy thought this was muddy back-breaking work, but that was just the beginning. Basket after basket of tiny plants was put on a flat bed wagon. The mule was hitched to the front, and Kate and Jimmy climbed up on the back. Moses coaxed the mule out to that field they had plowed. It slowly occurred to Jimmy that they were going to plant these little plants in those long rows! *This will take the rest of my life*, he thought. When he said this to Kate, she told him he would just have to learn to work fast. Kate and Moses seemed to enjoy the dazed look on his face.

Never could he have imagined such hard, boring muddy work. When Kate told him this was her garden, not a field of crops to be harvested for sale or trade, he could not even straighten his back to look at her. This field must be large enough to feed the entire county, if not the state. They were each working a row, and Jimmy was falling behind. The mule pulled the wagon load of baskets alongside the rows, standing patiently as they occasionally pulled a basket from the wagon. Moses worked with such easy fluid motions that Jimmy knew there must be a better method than what he was using, so he watched Moses for a few minutes. After adjusting his movements to simulate

Moses, some of the strain left his battered body, and the work moved along a little faster.

About an hour before dark, they ran out of the little plants. Since the plants could not be taken out of the cold frames and left overnight, they would stop working for the day. They loaded the last of the empty baskets onto the wagon and rode back to the barn. Between the unnatural positions Jimmy's back had been in, the repetitive movement of unused muscles, and the bouncing wagon trips, his body felt at least one hundred years old.

Before Kate went into the cabin to fix their supper, she insisted that Jimmy take a bath even though it was not Saturday night. Along one side of the barn, there was a shed with lots of tools hanging on the wall, and at the back end was a metal tub. It was not long enough to stretch out in, but if Jimmy wanted to soak a while, he would pull his knees up so his back could slide down.

Moses built a fire just outside the shed and heated buckets of water, which he poured into the tub. Jimmy stripped off his muddy clothes, hopped into the tub, and like a flash jumped back out. His screech was a lot like the cat in the barn loft.

Moses was watching with a big grin on his face. He showed Jimmy the pail of cold water and told him to add just a little to the tub. When the temperature was just below boiling, Jimmy eased back in. Never in his nineteen years had anything hurt so much and felt so good. He thought that if the water had not cooled off after half an hour or so, he would still be in that strange little tub. He could hear Moses splashing nearby but paid no attention. As he soaked one end and then the other, he wondered if Steve was working as hard as he was.

Moses returned bringing clean clothes and what looked like old flour sacks for towels. When Jimmy dried off, Moses pulled a brown bottle off a shelf and told him it would be a good idea to rub his back with liniment. You may have heard of liniment, but if you think it is like bath oil or lotion, you are way off base. Moses pulled the cork from the top and told Jimmy to take a sniff. So he took a deep breath. The odor was indescribable. Jimmy's stomach heaved, and his sinuses opened up instantly. His eyes watered until tears ran down his face and dripped off his chin. Moses turned him around and started rubbing his shoulders and back with this awful concoction.

When he could speak again, Jimmy asked him what was in this stuff. Moses told him it was really made for the horses and mules, but it was good for people too. By the time Moses finished rubbing, Jimmy was too weak to argue. They went into the cabin, ate more stew and corn bread, and hit the hay—literally. Is that where this saying comes from?

By the end of the week, Jimmy was working as fast as Moses and Kate. Either the hot baths or the liniment or maybe the stew was working wonders. He was getting muscles on his muscles.

On Friday Kate told Jimmy it was time to shear the sheep. They walked through a narrow patch of trees and climbed a fence into a field of grass with a tiny stream running across it. There were about twenty sheep including the lambs, nibbling and drinking from the stream and frolicking.

The field was enclosed by a wooden rail fence with vines growing on it. At the nearest corner was a covered shelter. Kate and Moses started herding the sheep into the shelter built into a corner of the field. Jimmy tried to help, but the sheep had other ideas. They scattered in all directions, baaing like they were being beaten. Jimmy took a quick turn and found himself on his butt, again. The smell from his shoes was strong and nasty. He was getting tired of looking like an idiot and smelling of poop. He grabbed a branch off a small tree and swung it around his head. The sheep thought he looked pretty crazy, so they ran into the shelter to hide. Apparently they believed there was safety in numbers.

The back and sides of the shelter were made of logs, with an opening in the front about five feet across. Moses put a rope around the neck of a big ewe and brought her just outside the entrance. There Kate proceeded to cut off big hunks of wool. She told Jimmy to pick it up and put it in the big baskets they had brought. He could barely keep up with her. When Kate finished, the ewe looked half the size she had been and stood there shivering until Moses untied her and pushed her away from the shed. This procedure went on until late afternoon without a break. All the sheep looked pitiful to Jimmy.

They hauled basket after basket back to the cabin, where Moses put a cauldron over a small fire, filled it with water, and started washing the fleece to remove dirt and sticks and who knows what else. Jimmy helped by squeezing the wool and spreading it on low tree branches to drip dry.

Kate was in the cabin, and just as they finished washing the wool, she called them to eat. Moses took his food and went outside to keep an eye on the cleaned fleece. Apparently the birds liked to steal bits and pieces for their nests.

As they ate, Kate explained that she would do something called *carding the wool* before she began to spin it into
yarn. Once again, Jimmy had no clue what she was talking
about, but he did not intend to ask because he did not
want to learn how this was done. Jimmy refilled the buckets from the well and closed the chickens into their smelly
home before he cleaned up and went to bed.

The chicken coop was near the barn but on the far
side, which was a good thing because the smell was really
bad. During the day, the chickens could roam around the
yard and woods, pecking at grasshoppers and bugs. Every
night they were closed up for their safety. After all, foxes
were still plentiful in the area. In the morning, Kate gathered the eggs, and they were soon used for breakfast and
baking. Jimmy was thankful for no longer being the person
to gather the eggs.

By Saturday Jimmy was considered trained enough to
plow a field without Moses to supervise. He even hitched
up the mule by himself. Just as he finished plowing the last
row, he heard his name called from the woods. It was Steve
with a big grin on his face. They grabbed each other and
slapped each other's back, and both talked at once. Finally
Jimmy shut up and found out what had happened to Steve.

What did you learn in this chapter?

_____

_____

_____

_____

_____

_____

_____

_____

_____

_____

_____

_____

Chapter 9

Steve's Story

Steve said that John Bell had taken him out the back of his house and across the field to a group of small cabins. At the last cabin, he took Steve inside and told the four young men that Steve was going to help with the spring planting. Then John left.

Steve said the four men just looked at him. He thought about leaving, but one of his new roommates stood up, reached behind him, and shut the door. Another man pulled up a stool and motioned Steve to join them around the fireplace. Three of the four were teenage boys, maybe sixteen or seventeen. The fourth looked a bit older, twenty or twenty-one. Steve sat with them, and they told him their names. Amos was the oldest one, and he was jet-black with the biggest muscles Steve had ever seen. The younger boys were tall and slim but looked strong too. They talked for a while, and Steve asked about the witch. They told him outrageous stories about last year's troubles, and Steve made no comment but tried to look suitably impressed. Amos had a pot of beans cooking over the fire and invited Steve to *et* with them. Amos pulled out a skillet, put it by the fire, and spooned a glob of grease into it. While the grease melted, Ned mixed some cornmeal, water, and an egg in a bowl. Then he cooked corn bread patties in the skillet. Ned and Amos said they were the only two who could cook anything fit to eat but would be glad to have Steve take a turn. When Steve admitted he had never cooked anything in his life, they sighed and said he could help clean up. Ned asked Steve where he was from. Steve thought it was safe to tell the truth and said he lived in Nashville.

Steve heard a lot of gossip from these young men about the strange happenings in and around the Bell family farm, but he was sure they were exaggerating. Apparently this invisible spirit talked and argued, slapped, pinched, and yanked covers and pillows off the beds. John Bell was the main target of the spirit, and he had aged greatly over the last two years. His hair was completely gray, and he had dark circles under his eyes. His daughter, Betsy, was often targeted too.

The next afternoon, Steve was told to take a load of firewood to the house. When he knocked on the back door, a large black woman opened the door and told him where to put the wood. While Steve stacked the wood, she was busy in the kitchen. Wonderful smells came from the big cast-iron cooking stove. Steve, being a friendly sort of guy, introduced himself and asked what she was cooking that smelled so good. Miss Lilah told him her name and said proudly that she was the cook for the Bell family. She said she was making blood pudding for dessert tonight. Steve's face must have given him away because Miss Lilah pulled out a chair and told him to sit. She poured a cup of water from a pitcher and insisted he drink and sit with her until he felt better. Steve really and truly did not want to know what was in that pudding, so he asked Miss Lilah how long she had been with the Bells.

That was all it took to get her talking. She had come from North Carolina with the family and had been with them for many years. She told Steve how hard it was to travel in wagons, herding the livestock and cooking over campfires, and in general how glad she was when they reached Adams. Then she described the land, building the barns and the house, and how much she enjoyed her work until just lately.

"The haunt started messing with the Bell family so bad, and everything had changed. Just last week, I was churning some cream into butter, but it would not turn."

Finally Miss Lilah got disgusted and decided the witch was causing the problem. She went to the stove, picked up a hot poker, and stuck it into the churn. Then she told Steve that she went to see Kate Batts on some pretense to check out a story she had heard. When she arrived, Kate had a strip of cloth wrapped around her hand and said she had burned it at the fireplace. This was convincing evidence to Miss Lilah that Kate was the witch and had been burned when Lilah stuck the hot poker into the churn. This logic seemed so strange to Steve that he decided he had better get back to work. He thanked Miss Lilah for the water and the visit and made his way back to the barnyard.

That night, as usual, there were more stories about the witch. One of the boys Steve was staying with was "stepping out" with a girl who worked inside the Bell home. Her name was Nell, and one of her duties was to start the fires in the various fireplaces in the house early in the morning. One morning Nell overslept and was late doing her duty. As she put a few pieces of kindling in one of the fireplaces, grumbling and mumbling and taking her time, the witch picked up a piece of wood and began hitting her over the head with it. Nell cried out as she was struck again and again. Another slave and one of the Bell children came running to the door in time to see the wood, seemingly by itself, strike the girl several more times. A voice called her a lazy, good-for-nothing slave. No one else was in the room. Nell was sobbing and could not be calmed down. She was sent back to her cabin for a rest. She did not over-sleep again.

Finally Steve told Jimmy that the slaves were gossiping that Andrew Jackson was coming to the Bell farm to see for himself if there was a real witch. He was supposed to be bringing a famous witch hunter who had silver bullets in his gun. This was really exciting for everyone. They wanted to be sure they were on hand to see the famous man.

It was nearly dark by then. Steve said he had to get back to his cabin for supper, so they planned to meet again at the edge of the woods every evening they could get away. Halfway back to Kate's cabin, Jimmy realized that Steve was no longer scratching his finger. The wart was gone.

What did you learn in this chapter?

_____

_____

_____

_____

_____

_____

_____

_____

_____

_____

_____

Chapter 10

Milk Will Never Taste the Same Again

In the second week, Jimmy learned to milk a cow. This was the most humiliating experience so far. Moses brought a bucket, stool, and a big black-and-white cow to the corner stall. He tied the cow to a post and put some feed in a trough for her. Moses asked Jimmy if he remembered watching him milk the cow the first morning they were there. Jimmy assured him he had watched carefully, so Moses went back to the other side of the barn.

Jimmy put the stool beside the cow and stood the bucket under her. Sitting on the little stool was awkward, but he folded his legs into position like an Indian. He reached for her teats and started to pull. The cow shifted a little, and her hoof came down on his foot. The pain was horrible. Moses heard him cry out, or maybe he heard his bones cracking, for he came running into the stall and pushed the cow off to the side. He shook his head and left Jimmy alone with the cow. Jimmy stood gingerly, putting a little weight on his aching foot before the cow shifted again and pushed him against the rough wall of the stall until he could not get a full breath. Jimmy yelled again, and Moses came over to push her away. This was getting really embarrassing. Jimmy finally got her situated and put the little stool beside her and the pail underneath, ready to start milking. He grabbed the first two teats and pulled. Nothing happened. Not one drop of milk came out. He had watched Moses and knew that you just pulled on the teats and milk flowed, so where was the milk?

He called Moses and told him that something was wrong with this cow. Moses left the cow he was milking and came to watch. This was getting to Jimmy—Moses watching him, the cow watching him, and Jimmy watching the bucket. Jimmy grabbed with both hands and pulled down on the teats, and a few measly drops of milk fell into the bucket. By this time, Kate had come in and was watching too. The cow was chewing some hay and had turned her head back toward Jimmy so she could see what was happening. After a few more pulls with little results, Kate took pity on Jimmy and showed him the right way to milk the cow. It took a few minutes to get the rhythm and hand movements coordinated, but milk that cow he did. He was as proud as when he first plowed a straight line with that ornery mule.

The bucket was about half full when the cow got bored. She stepped away from Jimmy. He shifted the bucket and stool closer to her and started milking again. She decided to move back to the original spot, and he tried to move the bucket, the stool, and himself all at the same time, but she was faster. He landed on his butt with the stool between his knees and the cow standing over him. The bucket of milk had survived, standing on the far side of the cow. He was congratulating himself when the cow decided to kick a few things out of her way. First she kicked his hip, then his head; then she kicked the bucket over. When Jimmy reached back to lever himself upright, his hand landed in something warm and squishy. He was afraid to look. The cow looked at him again; she looked at his hand and turned back to her feed, seemingly satisfied. Jimmy knew good and well that Moses heard the commotion, but he did not come running. For that Jimmy was extremely grateful.

By the time he got to his feet, washed his hands, and replaced the stool and bucket, he was a new man. No longer would he be dominated by a cow. When she pushed, he pushed back. When she kicked, he dodged. When she swished her tail, he ignored it. Finally the stream of milk tapered off to nothing, and the bucket was nearly full. Moses came back and stood admiring the bucket of milk. Then he looked behind him at Jimmy and saw the perfect handprint in the fresh cow patty. The change in his face was slight, but it is hard to be admired one minute and laughed at the next.

As they ate supper, Kate talked about selling a bull to a man in Kentucky. During the conversation, Jimmy learned that Kate had seven milk cows. Moses was milking six cows while he had milked one. That brought him down a notch or two.

What did you learn in this chapter?

_____

_____

_____

_____

_____

_____

_____

_____

_____

_____

_____

_____

Chapter 11

Tinker

Right after lunch the next day, they heard a loud clattering noise as someone came riding toward the cabin. They all went out to the front yard. The man riding in the front of the wagon was bigger than anyone Jimmy had seen around here. He was bearded, his hair long and in a tail down his back and his skin so brown he could have been an Indian. But his hair was a rusty red, and his eyes were blue. He whistled as he pulled the horses to a stop right in front of the cabin. Kate smiled happily and said, "Tinker, I was beginning to think you forgot about me."

"No way, ma'am. I brought your supplies just like you asked last fall." Tinker jumped down and tied the reins to the post. Moses came around the cabin with two buckets of water and poured them into the wooden trough, which seemed to make the horses very happy.

The wagon looked to Jimmy like a gypsy caravan wagon, without all the colors. But hanging from every possible place were pots, lids, tools, boxes, and some mysterious objects. Jimmy was fascinated. This must be an early version of Walmart, just on wheels.

Tinker climbed into the back and soon was pulling out the things Kate had ordered. There were two bolts of off-white fabric, a box with a new oil lamp, and packages wrapped in brown paper with *Kate* written on top. Moses began carrying them into the cabin and stacking them around the table. Kate and Tinker got seated, catching up on the gossip from his route through Kentucky, Tennessee, and Alabama. When Kate asked if he would like to stay for supper with them later, he accepted the invitation.

Tinker drove the wagon around the side of the cabin, unhooked his horses, and led them into the barn, talking all the way. Jimmy was amazed by his stories of other people, marriages, births, deaths, crops, and troubles. It seemed the man knew everyone for miles and miles around. Tinker rubbed his horses with an old sack, then brushed the burs and twigs from their coats. He checked their hooves and combed out their manes and tails. They were looking good when he finished. Jimmy watched with fascination and listened and laughed with Kate and Moses.

Kate decided to fix a big supper that night. Fried chicken was on the menu. Moses grabbed two chickens, chopped off their heads, and let them flop around the backyard until they died. This made Jimmy feel a lurch in his stomach. But that was nothing compared to what came next. Moses dunked the chickens in a big pot of boiling water, making a gut-wrenching odor fill the yard. He handed the chickens to Jimmy and told him to pull the feathers out, making sure to get the tiny pinfeathers, whatever that was. If you have never smelled wet chicken feathers, the odor is unlike any other bad smell in the world. It also lingers on your hands for days. Jimmy pulled feathers until he could not find anything else to pull out. He put the feathers in an old sack because Moses told him they would be put into pillows when they had enough. This idea was enough to boggle the mind of anyone with feather smell on their hands. How could anyone possibly sleep on something that smelled so bad?

Moses rinsed the chicken bodies in fresh water and took them inside to Kate. Jimmy washed and scrubbed his hands, but the faint smell of chicken feathers clung to his skin.

Jimmy came in and watched Kate cut off the feet of the chicken, yellow scales, black claws, and all. She tied them together with a piece of string and hung them on the wall beside the fireplace. That was the first time Jimmy noticed the other bunches of chicken feet hanging there. He could not stop himself from asking, "Don't tell me you are going to eat those chicken feet." Kate chuckled and said they were used for making broth, "We don't waste any part of the animals we kill for food. You take this bowl of innards out to Moses. He'd use them for fish bait."

More horrible smells rose from the bowl. Jimmy was totally grossed out. He wondered if he would ever be able to eat chicken again without remembering the smell of wet feathers and chicken guts.

Supper was delicious: fried chicken, potatoes, biscuits, and gravy, with a pie for dessert. Jimmy quickly got over his aversion to chicken.

Tinker slept in the back of his wagon. Early the next morning, he came to the barn to say goodbye to Moses and Jimmy. They helped him hitch up the horses and watched him roll away, clattering and whistling.

What did you learn in this chapter?

_____

_____

_____

_____

_____

_____

_____

_____

_____

_____

_____

_____

_____

Chapter 12

Is It Love?

As Jimmy lay in the loft one night, he heard the sound of footsteps coming from below. They were sneaky footsteps. He sat up as quietly as he could. Someone was climbing the ladder! A girl's head appeared near his feet. It was the girl he had glimpsed so long ago in the cave. She came up, and they talked. Her name was Priscilla, and she had been watching him from the woods for several days. He hoped she had not seen him the day he learned to plow and wisely decided not to ask her. Priscilla said she lived across the river and asked if Jimmy could swim. He assured her he could and was invited to join her for a swim the next afternoon. They planned to meet at a place called the *deep hole*, which sounded a bit strange since the Red River was shallow. Priscilla told him most places in the river were not deep enough for swimming, so the one area that was deeper had been dubbed the *deep hole*. Priscilla said she had to get on home and would see him the next afternoon. Before he drifted into sleep, he wondered if Priscilla could be Kate's daughter.

The next morning at breakfast, he asked Kate about her daughter. She gave him a look that would freeze a fire and told him her daughter lived in Louisville, and she was none of his business. That left Jimmy wondering who the girl could be. Since she was not one of the Bell family and had not been at the church or the dinner on the ground, it seemed strange to have seen her in the cave and then in the barn. But that did not stop him from meeting her for a swim late that afternoon.

Priscilla was a little vague about her family when Jimmy asked her. But she was very pretty and handled him like a pretty girl usually handles an interested man, young or old. She told him to just call her *Prissy*, so he did. They swam partially dressed, then lay on the grassy bank to dry in the sunshine. Jimmy thought he had never seen such a beautiful girl. She wore no makeup and needed none. Her hair was black, shining in waves down her back to her waist.

They met almost every evening for the next two weeks, and soon they were thinking about love. Finally he had to tell her that his visit here was nearly over. She began to cry, and he held her, not knowing what to say or do. Jimmy was feeling pretty bad about leaving, too, but he knew he did not want to live here at this time, and Steve would need his help to get free so they could make their way home. She begged him to stay with her. He could only give her kisses and hold her.

What did you learn in this chapter?

_____

_____

_____

_____

_____

_____

_____

_____

_____

_____

_____

_____

Chapter 13

The Witch Hunter

Andrew Jackson was on his way to the Bell farm! Steve would see him there, but Jimmy probably would not, so he slipped away to watch for him. The dirt road from Nashville was bordered by woods along the edge of the Bell farm, running along beside the river part of the way. He was determined to at least get a glimpse of this man, so he found a spot in the woods where he could see the road for a good distance. He had been perched in a tree for about an hour when he saw a wagon headed his way. There were four mules pulling the wagon and two men in the seat, talking and laughing. About fifty feet before they reached Jimmy, the wagon stopped. The men yelled at the mules, and one of them snapped a whip at them, but they did not move the wagon. Jimmy could see them straining against their collars, trying to pull, but the wagon did not budge. Finally the men climbed down and checked the wagon but could not find anything that would stop the wheels from rolling. Eventually they climbed back onto the wagon seat, and one of them picked up the reins. Jimmy nearly fell out of the tree when a familiar woman's voice came from the air above and said, "You can go on now, General. I'll see you later." The mules pulled again, and the wagon rolled on.

Jimmy stayed in the tree for a little while, wondering if the spirit was watching him. After the stories he had heard, he did not want her mad at him. In fact, he did not want her to even notice his existence.

That night, Steve did not come to the woods to talk to Jimmy. Prissy did not show up either. Jimmy was left to wonder.

What did you learn in this chapter?

_____

_____

_____

_____

_____

_____

_____

_____

_____

_____

_____

_____

_____

Chapter 14

The Outhouse Experience

The next day was Sunday, so Jimmy dressed in clean clothes and joined Kate for breakfast. After church services, everyone stood around talking, and he was able to meet Steve behind the outhouse.

Has anyone described the outhouse experience for you? It was powerful, to say the least. Three weeks ago, when Jimmy first asked Moses where the bathroom was, Moses pointed to a small building near the woods behind the barn. Jimmy thought it was too small to be anything but maybe storage for small tools, but he went. The wooden door had a cutout of a quarter moon, which he thought was funny. Jimmy pulled the handle to open the door. Something pulled back. He pulled harder, and the door opened.

Now bear in mind that this was a sunny day. The building was built tight, probably to keep small animals out, so not much air circulated in there. The only feature was a wooden bench with a round hole cut in it, about eight by ten inches. The odor was incredible. Jimmy's head started swimming, and his stomach clenched. Moses advised him to hold the door open for a few minutes to allow some fresh air to get inside. Jimmy held the door open and backed as far away as possible. When he could wait no longer, he went inside. On the end of the bench seat was an old basket filled with corncobs and husks. How he longed for the clean tile bathroom and soft toilet paper back at his dorm. He promised himself that if he could ever get back home, he would never ever complain about cleaning the bathroom.

As he sat on the rough wooden seat, being very careful due to the possibility of splinters, he felt something moving in his hair. He grabbed some corncobs and swiped them across his head. Nothing fell off. A minute later, he felt something crawling across his back and shoulder. He could not sit still any longer, and with a shriek, he opened the door and popped out. His britches were around his ankles so he fell, face first, on the ground. Since he was still shrieking, his mouth was filled with dirt. He bit the dust. Moses came trotting over from the barn and took a long look. Jimmy's toes, knees, shoulders, arms, and face were touching the ground. His middle was up in the air. Moses was trying hard not to laugh, but his brown face was turning red. He helped Jimmy up and asked what had happened. While Jimmy pulled up his pants, he told Moses about the thing crawling up his back and onto his shoulders. Moses decided to take a look inside. He pulled the door open and took a quick look before letting the door shut. Then he asked Jimmy if he was afraid of snakes. Jimmy said he had never seen one in person. Moses walked to the barn and brought back a pitchfork and a shovel. He said, "Have you ever heard of a copperhead?" Jimmy knew that was a poisonous snake and said so. Moses asked if he would like to see one. It was slowly dawning on Jimmy that a copperhead had been crawling up his back, and he started to shiver all over. Moses opened the door, slowly put the pitchfork inside, and brought it back out with the snake wrapped around the tines. Jimmy, being a little bit smart, backed away several steps. Moses gently laid the pitchfork on the ground and looked at Jimmy. His face must have been white or maybe green because he felt like he would throw up his breakfast. The snake slowly uncoiled itself and started to slither away. Moses took the shovel and slammed it into the ground, right through the middle of the snake. The snake's mouth opened, and out came about a dozen tiny copperhead snakes. They were moving so fast Moses did not have time to kill them. Moses told Jimmy how the baby snakes lived inside the mother snake's body; she carried them around that way. This was definitely more than he wanted to know on the subject. While he threw up into the weeds beside the outhouse, Moses checked inside to see if there were any more snakes. When he came around to check on Jimmy, Moses told him he could go back in and finish his business now. Jimmy told Moses he would probably never need to go again, but if he did, it would be in the woods.

Anyway, back to meeting Steve after church. This is the story Steve told him.

What did you learn in this chapter?

_____

_____

_____

_____

_____

_____

_____

_____

_____

_____

_____

_____

Chapter 15

Andrew Jackson Was Here

Andrew Jackson and the *witch hunter* arrived at the Bells' house about supper time. When they came in the door, the witch hunter was carrying a rifle. The Bells invited them to join them for supper, and they all had a big time talking about the witch and their trials and tribulations with her. The witch hunter continued bragging about his experiences getting rid of troublesome spirits. After supper they retired to the parlor to await the arrival of the witch. The witch hunter continued bragging about his powers and kept his rifle in his lap. It was loaded with one silver bullet, which he claimed was necessary in his line of work. The witch did not show up, and everyone was getting tired and bored.

Just as they were thinking of going to bed, footsteps crossed the wooden floor. Jackson and the witch hunter looked around, following the sound of the steps. No one was there. The steps went to the front of the fireplace and stopped. The witch spoke, daring the witch hunter to shoot. He aimed at the place the voice came from and pulled the trigger. Nothing happened. He tried again, but the gun would not fire. He was knocked from his chair. Everyone heard the slap as something hit his face. He jumped up and ran around the room, screaming, "Oh, Lord, the devil's got me by the nose!" He ran out the door and raced down the road. Andrew Jackson was laughing so hard he was holding his sides. From the air came the sounds of a woman laughing. The witch thought it was pretty funny too.

What did you learn in this chapter?

_____

_____

_____

_____

_____

_____

_____

_____

_____

_____

_____

_____

Chapter 16

Roots and Dyes

Early the next morning, Kate led Jimmy to a raggedy garden plot south of the barn. He thought the plants were all weeds, and he was going to be told to pull and dig them out. Instead, Kate stopped over a group of plants, about ten inches tall. She told Jimmy to help her pull out the roots. As they filled Kate's basket, she explained she needed bloodroot to dye her yarn, and this plant would make a rust color. She planned to dry these roots in the root cellar and use it in the fall.

When the basket was full, they walked on through the weeds. Kate pointed out several plants and told Jimmy the colors each would give her yarn. Queen Anne's lace made a pale green, the peppermint a dark brownish green, and St. John's wort a golden yellow. The inner bark of the hedge apple tree gave a pale yellow.

Their second basket was soon filled with St. John's wort flowers and leaves. As she talked, they came to a patch of taller plants, which Kate identified as elecampane. They dug up the roots, which Kate said would yield blues or purple.

Jimmy did not see how this could be possible, but he found out it was true. They returned to the cabin, where Moses was tending two fires, each with a big black cauldron in the middle. Steam was rising into the warm morning air. Kate told Jimmy to draw a bucket of water from the well and wash the dirt from the roots, keeping them in separate piles. "Don't mix them together, or the color will not be true," she told him as she went into the cabin. He did as he was told.

Moses gathered several buckets from the barn and told Jimmy to fill them at the well. About twenty feet from the back corner of the cabin was a stone circle about four feet tall. A wooden frame reached above and across the opening in the middle. Jimmy tied a bucket to the rope, which went through a pulley at the top. He let out more and more rope until he heard the bucket splash into the water far below. After a minute, to let the bucket fill, he pulled the rope until the bucket reached the top, and he untied it and set it on the rocks. He repeated the action until all the buckets were full.

Kate came out with a knife and showed Jimmy how to peel the bark off the roots and cut them into small pieces. When he completed the task, she put the pieces into two small iron pots and set them at the edge of the fire. The water was soon steaming, and the smells were strange.

They all took a break for some lunch. Kate had brought four large baskets of yarn from the back room. The yarn was in big loops, loosely tied together at one end. Jimmy was getting interested, but he was still mad at Kate for loaning Steve to John Bell, so he did not ask her any questions while he ate. Moses brought his plate to the door and passed it to Kate.

They gathered around the fires. Kate used an old piece of cloth to strain the liquids from the small pots into the big cauldrons. Jimmy brought the baskets of yarn from the kitchen and put two baskets by each fire. Moses measured some white powder into each cauldron.

Kate began dropping the yarn into the cauldrons and stirring them around with a stick. Jimmy was amazed to see the yarn soaking up the colors. The longer they were in the dye bath, the darker they became. Kate handed Jimmy a stick and told him to fish the yarn out, one bunch at a time, and lay it over the rope stretched between two trees at the edge of the yard. When all the colorful yarn was out, dripping into the grass, they added more yarn to the pots. The color of the yarn was a little lighter this time.

Moses let the fires die down when they had finished all the yarn. He told Jimmy that when the things cooled down, they would dump the dye in the woods so it would not leak into their well water.

Jimmy thought they were through, but no. Remember all the buckets of water? Kate had Jimmy and Moses bring them closer to the line of dripping yarn. They proceeded to dip the yarn into a bucket, squeeze it out, dip it into the next bucket, squeeze it out, and finally dip it into the third bucket. When they squeezed the yarn this time, the water ran clear. They hung the bundles of yarn up to dry. Again Jimmy thought this chore was done, and again he was wrong.

He helped Moses hitch the mule to the wagon and guide it over to the big pots. Using old sacks to protect their hands, they loaded the big cauldrons into the back of the wagon. Moses filled two buckets with water and put them on the wagon. Moses guided the mule, and Jimmy rode in the back to help keep their load steady. There were no lids, so the warm liquid sloshed about. Jimmy kept one hand on each cauldron, thinking to keep them from sliding out. He forgot Kate's warning to be careful not to get the dye on him or his clothes. Sure enough, the liquid soon covered his hands and arms, then his shoes and the legs of his overalls. It was running along the cracks in the planks and soon reached his upper legs and butt. When Moses halted the mule just inside the woods, Jimmy got out.

Moses started laughing again when he saw the stains all over Jimmy. Blue covered his left hand and arm and ran up the back of his leg and one side of his bottom. Yellow was on his right hand and arm and ran up that leg to his bottom. Where the colors met in the middle of his backside, there was a wide greenish stripe. Jimmy pushed his hair back and rubbed his face. That made Moses laugh more.

Eventually they unloaded the cauldrons and tipped them over into the dirt. Moses poured a bucket of water into each one, sloshed it around, and poured it out. They put the cauldrons on the wagon and turned through the trees to return to the barn. Moses chuckled all the way.

The sun was going down, casting shadows across the yard. Jimmy thought about meeting Steve at the edge of the field but decided he would rather eat supper and go to sleep. Kate had their meal ready and called out to them to wash up. That's when Jimmy realized his hands and arms were going to keep their colorful glory. All the scrubbing with the rough soap only lightened the colors a little bit. When he went inside and sat at the table, Kate got a look at him. His face had a blue smear across the forehead, his blond hair turned blue on one side, and his hands and arms were red from scrubbing, but still blue and yellow. She laughed until she had to sit down.

What did you learn in this chapter?

_____

_____

_____

_____

_____

_____

_____

_____

_____

_____

_____

_____

Chapter 17

Medicine

A few days later, Kate had Moses and Jimmy go to a small cave on the side of the hill away from the river. There was a wooden door with a bar across it to keep the animals out. Inside were rough wooden shelves filled with baskets and jugs. Jimmy felt like he was in a refrigerated storage room because the temperature was so cool. Moses rummaged around a bit and handed Jimmy two of the jugs with large round corks in the tops. Moses picked up three big flat baskets of dried leaves and flowers. They locked up and took their booty back to the cabin.

Once again Moses brought a small cauldron from the barn, but this time, he took it into the kitchen. There Kate opened the two jugs and poured a smelly oily glob of something into the cauldron. In spite of himself, Jimmy was interested. As the fire heated the white globs, the smell increased until Jimmy had to ask what was going on. Kate said, "We're making medicine for cuts and bruises, called a *balm*." When the stuff melted, she began throwing in cups of herbs. These are comfrey leaves, these are calendula leaves, and these here are lavender flowers to make it smell good. Of course, Jimmy thought this mess could never smell anywhere near good, but he kept his opinion to himself. After an hour or so, Kate took the cauldron down from the fire and took it to the backyard to cool. In another small pot, Moses was stirring beeswax. Kate had Jimmy hold an old sack over a third pot and strained the leaves and flowers out of the mysterious smelly mess. Then Moses poured the beeswax into the pot and stirred and stirred. Sure enough, it did smell better.

Kate brought seven small wide-mouthed jugs to the fire and instructed Jimmy to dip the balm into the jugs. As each one filled up, she would put a cork top on it and set it aside. Then Jimmy and Moses hauled the baskets and the jugs of balm back to the coolness of the little cave. Jimmy had no idea how soon he would be needing this strange medicine.

That night the rains came with plenty of lightning and thunder. It was hard to sleep with all the noise and flashing lights.

While eating breakfast the next morning, Kate told them there was a leak in her roof, and she wanted them to fix it. The roof was made of cedar planks called *shakes*, and the storm had blown a few off. Since Jimmy was not skilled with an axe, he watched as Moses cut down a cedar tree. Together they dragged it to the edge of the woods near the yard. Then Moses sent Jimmy to the barn for the two-man saw. Each held the handle at their end of the saw and proceeded to cut through the trunk of the tree. This took a long time and yet another set of muscles to use and strain. Jimmy said nothing for fear Moses would rub the liniment on him again.

Jimmy took the axe and cut the limbs from the trunk. His arms and back began to feel abused, but not enough to chance another liniment rub.

Moses took over the axe and chopped a section of the trunk about twenty inches from their cut. He stood that hunk of wood on the stump in the backyard and proceeded to chop long slices of wood to make the shingles. Every time he cut one slice, he turned the wood over so he ended up with slices that were all evenly thick.

That afternoon Jimmy and Moses were patching the roof of the cabin when Jimmy lost his footing and slid off the roof, landing on the washstand and falling to the ground. Moses climbed down and offered a hand to help Jimmy up. Since he was not breathing yet, Jimmy stayed put. Eventually he was able to take a deep breath and crawled to the cabin wall to steady himself.

Kate came from the chicken house and looked him over. He was definitely going to have lots of bruises and was dreading the word *liniment*. But Kate told Moses to get some balm from the little cave. Once again Jimmy was soaking in the strange little tub. Moses brought the flour sacks to dry him off, then rubbed the balm on his chest, back, and the backs of his legs. Jimmy rubbed the stuff on his upper arms and the front of his legs. He did not mention that his ribs were the most damaged place on his body, still fearing the "liniment treatment."

What did you learn in this chapter?

_____

_____

_____

_____

_____

_____

_____

_____

_____

_____

_____

_____

Chapter 18

The Witch Throws a Party

A few days later, Steve told Jimmy the strangest story about the witch. It seemed the witch had been raiding local stills and was drunk. She was heard yelling and cursing all around Adams. She would spit on the slaves, pull covers off sleeping children, turn furniture over, and pinch and slap people. Several local moonshiners complained that their stills were being raided. That was the first and only time they ever heard of a spirit getting drunk. Apparently alcohol had the same effect on spirits that it had on some people they knew, making them mean and hateful.

To make things worse, the witch brought some friends home with her for a party. They drank and made lots of noise, yelling and laughing and screaming at people. Finally they introduced themselves as Blackdog (a female with a harsh voice), Mathematics and Cyprocryphy (who sounded like females), and Jerusalem (who sounded like a young boy). This party went on night after night. All this time, they were invisible. A few days later, they were seen.

One of the Bell daughters, Esther, had married and lived nearby. She was going to the henhouse to gather eggs when she noticed a woman slowly walking down the lane. She called a greeting, but the woman ignored her. She called out again, but the woman continued her slow progress down the lane. Esther's sister, Betsy Bell, was visiting, so Esther called Betsy to come outside. Soon four more people had joined the old woman on the lane: two young women, an older woman, and a boy. They turned away to walk through a lot bordered by small trees. There they pulled the saplings over and began to swing on them. Esther's husband, Bennett Porter, came home, and Esther pointed out the strange group to him. He could see the trees bending and straightening but could not see anyone. He handed his rifle to his wife and told her to shoot. She could not do it and instead offered to tell him where to aim. There was a large log near the edge of the lot, and the five spirits ducked behind it. They seemed to take turns popping up for a look and quickly hiding again. Esther told her husband to aim at a spot over a large knothole in the log, and he fired. The bullet hit the top edge of the log, making all the spirits disappear. Esther and her family ran over to see what was behind the log but found nothing at all.

When the witch spoke at the Bells' home later that night, she complained that the bullet had broken Jerusalem's arm. She was quite angry about it.

After that the witch seemed to be angry all the time. She tormented Betsy Bell, the other Bell children, and more often John Bell. She seemed determined to worry him to death.

Their time was running out. Steve and Jimmy wanted very much to help but had no idea what to do.

What did you learn in this chapter?

_____

_____

_____

_____

_____

_____

_____

_____

_____

_____

_____

_____

Chapter 19

Time to Go

The night of the full moon finally arrived. Kate told Jimmy to be ready after dark. He washed and dressed in the clothes he came in and waited inside the barn. Soon he heard men shouting and dogs barking and knew that Steve had *escaped*. Kate took Jimmy down the path toward the cave. When Steve ran up behind them, she led them both down the trail to the mouth of the cave. She told them to wait outside the entrance and keep quiet, and she would return to tell them what to do. Kate went back up the path to send the searchers on down the river.

It seemed like hours before they heard someone rushing down the path. Prissy threw herself into Jimmy's arms, crying and laughing. She was determined to go with him. Jimmy did not know if it was possible but agreed to try. Steve looked doubtful but was happy just to be getting out of there.

They waited for Kate. The moon rose slowly across the sky. Kate had told them that the moon would be truly full just before dawn. Prissy edged back into the mouth of the cave. Jimmy called her to come back because Kate had told them to wait outside, but she went on into the darkness. Jimmy and Steve went after her, stumbling on the rocks. They could hear Prissy ahead of them and wondered how she could see where she was going. Steve kept pulling on Jimmy, trying to tell him to wait for Kate, but Jimmy wanted to get Prissy outside. The murmuring noise in the back of the cave seemed much louder now. Steve said he was going back out and begged Jimmy to come with him. Some of the bats were returning to the cave, and when one landed on Jimmy's head, he decided Steve was right—they should wait outside. They stumbled back through the hanging vines and sat on a boulder. They could no longer hear the men and dogs, so Kate much have been successful in diverting them.

Without a sound, Kate walked up to them. Jimmy tried to tell her about Prissy, but she shushed him saying the men were coming back this way. She told them to be quiet and follow her. She held an oil lamp in one hand, put out her other hand for Jimmy, and told Steve to take Jimmy's other hand. They went once again into the first passageway and across the round room. There she stationed them just inside the second passage and told them to wait. Jimmy held Steve's arm and looked down the curving passage for Prissy, but there was not enough light to see very far. They stood frozen and waited.

Kate was gone. How she had disappeared without making a sound was beyond them. Now they had two women missing inside the cave. They listened to the water dripping and the murmuring of voices coming from the back passage. Then they heard again the sound of a rock beating on the walls of the cave. *BAM, BAM, BAM!* To tell the truth, Jimmy did not know if he was shaking or if it was Steve, but they were rooted to the floor and shivering like trees in a high wind. Then the air rushed by them, and the glowing cloud came down the passage toward them. They ran.

When they jumped through the vines and landed on the grass, they fell right on top of their sleeping bags. By the time they untangled themselves from each other, the moon was almost gone, and they were in the dark.

What did you learn in this chapter?

_____

_____

_____

_____

_____

_____

_____

_____

_____

_____

_____

_____

Chapter 20

Home again

"Look up that way!" Steve shouted. Up the river, they could see the outlines of trees and a little shine on the water. Their gear was beside the tents, and the canoe was on the gravel bar. They were back!

Steve started grabbing their gear and told Jimmy to bring the sleeping bags or just leave them. They made their way down the cliff and threw all their stuff into the canoe. As they paddled out into the water, Jimmy looked back at the cave. Just outside the entrance stood Prissy, waving goodbye. He wanted to go back for her, but she walked back into the cave.

They paddled and floated on down the river, exhausted. They did not talk much and just looked and listened. Far above they could see the tiny lights of a jet airplane. They floated under a concrete bridge and heard a car crossing above them. They were hungry, but there was no way they were stopping to dig out the food. Jimmy was glad to find granola bars in an outside pocket of his backpack, which they munched as they floated.

The Red River Canoe Rental sign on the riverbank was the most beautiful sight they had ever seen, peeling paint and all. The sun was just lighting the sky to the east, and they wanted to shout "We're back!" but did not have the energy. They pulled the canoe to the bank and unloaded their gear. Walking toward them was Mike, singing and smiling. When he asked them how they liked the trip, they were both speechless for a minute. They looked at each other and burst into laughter. Mike helped them carry their gear to the car and invited them to come back again. They shook hands with him and piled into the car.

Jimmy was thinking of Prissy. She was as much a mystery as their time travel was. He realized he did not know much about her or exactly where she lived. She seemed familiar with the cave, enough to be able to get around inside without a lantern. Why did she separate from them if she really wanted to go with Jimmy back to his time? Maybe she knew it was not possible for her to leave. This was another puzzle which he could not answer. It felt like they had nothing but puzzles left. Steve argued that they had learned a lot about living in the early 1800s.

Jimmy remembered Steve's problem with the wart on his little finger. It was obviously gone, so he asked Steve how he got rid of it. Steve said, "It's the strangest thing. The cook at the Bells' house told me to rub the juice from a dandelion stem on it two or three times a day for a couple of days and it would disappear. She was right. Three days later, it was gone."

As they drove south, Jimmy asked Steve if he wanted to go canoeing again. "Absolutely, positively, no way."

What did you learn in this chapter?

_____

_____

_____

_____

_____

_____

_____

_____

_____

_____

_____

About the Author

In 1990, Joy Kieffer married and moved to Adams, Tennessee. They lived on the farm called the Bell Witch Cave Farm, and she helped her husband's parents by giving tours of the cave. At first, she did not believe any of the stories they told her about the strange happenings there, but so many unexplainable events soon her wondering. By the time they sold the farm and moved a few miles away, she was convinced that there are many things that our science cannot explain. The first experience was of loud stomping footsteps coming from the back of the cave, getting closer and closer to them. They had just unlocked the gate and knew that no one could be there but the two of them. Nevertheless, they left quickly and locked the gate.

Some of the stories she was told are incorporated into this book. She hopes you enjoy it.

Printed in the USA
CPSIA information can be obtained
at www.ICGtesting.com
LVHW051642110823
754975LV00013B/33